D0791452

Video Mischief

AMANDA GODFREOW

By Mary Packard
Illustrated by Tom Tierney

A GOLDEN BOOK • NEW YORK
Western Publishing Company, Inc., Racine, Wisconsin 53404

Holly Pierce was interviewing the hot new rock group, Jem and the Holograms, on TV.

"Catch this," said Pizzazz, lead singer of her own group, the Misfits.

The other band members, Roxy and Stormer, stared at the TV screen in disbelief.

"I hear you've just finished your new album," said Holly. "Can you give us a sneak preview?"

"We can't do that," said Jem. "But here's a hint. The album is called *Animal Attraction*. We're off to Kenya tonight to shoot some videos."

"Are they for real?" said Pizzazz.

"We're off to Kenya," said Roxy, mimicking Jem.

"The Holograms aren't going to show us up this time," said Pizzazz. "If it weren't for their last album, we would have won the Gold Record Award for *Riot in the Streets*."

"We've got to do something to mess up their trip,"
said Stormer.

"And those videos," added Roxy.

"That's right, ladies," said Pizzazz. "We're going to
Kenya, too. And when Jem sees us, she'd better
watch out!"

The Misfits hurried to pack their bags.

As the Holograms drove home from the TV station, Jem pressed a finger to one of her magic earrings. "Show's over, Synergy," she said.

With the help of Synergy, a holographic computer, Jem was instantly transformed into Jerrica Benton, head of Starlight Music.

"We're home," Aja said to Shana and Kimber, the other members of the Holograms. They went inside Starlight Mansion.

Rio, Jerrica's boyfriend and the group's manager, was there. He was in the dark about Jerrica's double identity. "Where's Jem?" he asked. "You all have to be at the airport in an hour."

"Jem had to wrap things up at the studio," said Jerrica. "She'll meet you at the airport."

"Okay," said Rio. "I'd better get going. I have to make sure that all the instruments get on the plane. See you when I get back, Jerrica." He headed for his car.

On the way to the airport, Jerrica touched her earring again and said, "Show's on, Synergy." Like magic, she was transformed into Jem.

After pushing their way through crowds of fans, Jem and the Holograms were finally on their way to Africa.

But among the passengers on the plane were the Misfits, traveling in disguise!

"Welcome to Kenya," said Howard Sands, the video director. He'd met the group at the airport, and was taking them to his private game preserve.

Along the way they stopped to look at some animals that were grazing in the grass.

"Get those mice out of here!" shouted Howard. But it was too late. The lions had already forgotten about being video stars and were playing cat and mouse instead—with *mechanical* mice!

"Who's got the weird sense of humor?" fumed Rio. He looked behind a camera and saw Pizzazz, holding a bag and giggling.

"Pizzazz, what are you doing here?" Rio shouted.
"Uh-oh," said Pizzazz, and she took off into the
woods. Rio followed her and watched as she
disappeared into a tent not far from the set.

"That's a day's work down the drain," said Jem. "And we have to be back home for a concert the day after tomorrow."

"Don't worry," soothed Rio. "All we have to do is shoot the videos tonight."

Jem's eyes lit up. "And we'll let the Misfits think we're shooting tomorrow!"

"Right," said Rio, and he headed for the Misfits' tent.

"What brings you here, Rio?" Pizzazz asked,
trying hard to sound sweet.

"I came to beg you to keep off the set tomorrow," said
Rio. "Our time is running out, and we have to shoot
both videos in one day. Can't you see the bind we're in?"

Pizzazz only smiled. Her plan was working even
better than she thought.

That night, everything went perfectly. The high-powered floodlights made the set as bright as day. The chimps and lions were on their best behavior. Best of all, there were no surprise appearances from Pizzazz and the Misfits!

"Cut!" called Howard when the shoot was over. "Nice work, everybody."

They were all so busy celebrating, they didn't notice Leo wander off into the woods.

Suddenly, the sound of screams sent everyone
running toward the Misfits' tent.

"What's going on?" cried Rio.

"L-look!" sputtered Pizzazz. She pointed to Leo, who
had found a comfortable spot for a nap.

"Help!" wailed Roxy. "Lions are dangerous!"

"Not this one," said Jem. "He's as tame as a kitten. But you won't have to worry about 'wild' animals anymore. Tonight we finished shooting both videos, so there's nothing left for you to mess up."

Pizzazz turned to Rio and said, "But you said you were shooting tomorrow."

"Can't always believe everything you hear," Rio told her.

The next day Jem and the Holograms flew home. Jem slipped away for a moment and pressed a finger to her earring. "Show's over, Synergy," she said softly. Now she was Jerrica Benton again.

"The videos look great," Rio said when he saw Jerrica, "but you'll never guess what happened on the set."

"Tell me all about it," Jerrica replied with a mischievous grin.